To all the dreamers
—T.A.-N.

For Juana and Ulises,
my daydreamers
—N.C.

NANCY PAULSEN BOOKS
An imprint of Penguin Random House LLC, New York

Text copyright © 2021 by Talia Aikens-Nuñez
Illustrations copyright © 2021 by Penguin Random House LLC

Nancy Paulsen Books is a trademark of Penguin Random House LLC.

Visit us online at penguinrandomhouse.com

Library of Congress Cataloging-in-Publication Data
Names: Aikens-Nuñez, Talia, author. | Colombo, Natalia, illustrator.
Title: Small nap, little dream / Talia Aikens-Nuñez; illustrated by Natalia Colombo.
Description: New York: Nancy Paulsen Books, [2021] | Summary: "A naptime story that introduces
simple Spanish vocabulary as it describes all the fun things in a child's day"—Provided by publisher.
Includes glossary of Spanish words.
Identifiers: LCCN 2020019295 | ISBN 9780525517825 (hardcover) | ISBN 9780525517849 (ebook) |
ISBN 9780525517832 (ebook)
Subjects: CYAC: Naps (Sleep)—Fiction. | Spanish language—Vocabulary—Fiction.
Classification: LCC PZ7.1.A355 Sue 2021 | DDC [E]—dc23
LC record available at https://lccn.loc.gov/2020019295

Manufactured in China by RR Donnelley Asia Printing Solutions Ltd.
ISBN 9780525517825
1 3 5 7 9 10 8 6 4 2

Design by Marikka Tamura
Text set in Cooper Std
The illustrations for this book were made with
colored pencils and acrylics.

Small Nap, Little Dream

By Talia Aikens-Nuñez

Illustrated by Natalia Colombo

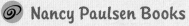 Nancy Paulsen Books

Glossary
of
Spanish Words

cuerpo (KWEHR-po): body

estómago (ehs-STOH-mah-go): stomach

manos (MAH-nos): hands

mi (mee): my

mis (meehs): my (plural)

ojos (OH-hos): eyes

pies (PEE-ehs): feet

piernas (pee-EHR-nahs): legs

siesta (see-EHS-tah): nap

sueñito (swehn-YEE-tow): little dream

Look at me RUN.
Mis pies go fast!

Look at me JUMP.

Mis piernas are strong!

Look at me CLIMB.
Mis brazos work hard!

Look at me CLAP.
Mis manos are loud!

Look at me LAUGH.
Mi estómago shakes!

Look at me READ.
Mis ojos explore!

Look at me YAWN.
Siesta time!

We love small naps
and little dreams.

Sueñito . . .

Look, I'm AWAKE!
Mi cuerpo rested!

We love to nap.
We love to play.
We love to dream.
Sueñito.